PUFFIN BOOKS

The Snowman

MICHAEL MORPURGO
The
Snowman

A new story inspired by the original tale by

RAYMOND BRIGGS

Illustrated by Robin Shaw

PUFFIN

PUFFIN BOOKS

UK | USA | Canada | Ireland | Australia
India | New Zealand | South Africa

Puffin Books is part of the Penguin Random House group of companies
whose addresses can be found at global.penguinrandomhouse.com.

www.penguin.co.uk   www.puffin.co.uk   www.ladybird.co.uk

Text by Michael Morpurgo
Illustrations by Robin Shaw
Text and illustrations copyright © Snowman Enterprises Ltd 2018
THE SNOWMAN™ Snowman Enterprises Ltd
The animated film THE SNOWMAN, produced in 1982, is based on the book
The Snowman by Raymond Briggs, first published by Hamish Hamilton in 1978
Licensed by Penguin Books Ltd

004

Typeset in Dante
Printed and bound in Great Britain by Clays Ltd, Elcograf S.p.A.

A CIP catalogue record for this book is available from the British Library

ISBN: 978-0-241-35241-0

All correspondence to:
Puffin Books
Penguin Random House Children's
80 Strand, London WC2R ORL

For Mac and Edna and Seonaid and Stuart.
Remembering all the happy Christmases – MM

The Snowman

James

Mum and Dad

Bertie

Father Christmas

Grandma

Snowmen

Chapter One

Once upon a Christmas there was a little boy called James. James lived with his mum and dad, and Bertie, their sheepdog, on a farm deep in the countryside. They had cows and pigs and sheep and hens and ducks and geese, and they had a horse they called Big, and a donkey they called Little.

★ THE SNOWMAN ★

When James looked out of his bedroom window – which he did a lot because that's where he did most of his dreaming – he could see his dad's shed at the bottom of the garden, the weedy duck pond, his mum's vegetable patch, the swing, and the trampoline that Grandma had given him the Christmas before.

And beyond the garden hedge he could see fields – Oak Tree Field was his favourite because that was where the owl hooted from. There were so many fields on the farm, and hedges and trees – more than he could count – and a river running along the bottom of the valley like a silver ribbon. And beyond the river, high on the horizon, were the rolling hills of the moor.

★ THE SNOWMAN ★

Grandma always came for Christmas. She often said – and she did say things too often sometimes – that mostly you couldn't see the hills around the farm because it was raining; but if you could see them, that meant it was going to rain soon, or snow. Grandma, who lived in a town, didn't mind the rain and snow as much as the birds that woke her up early every morning, or the smell of pigs and cows that James often brought back into the house on his wellies when he had been out on the farm. She didn't much like green either, and of course there was a lot of green about in the countryside.

What Grandma liked best was when James had had a bath and was all nice and clean, and in bed in his nice clean jimjams – as Grandma always called his pyjamas. She loved sitting on his bed and telling him a story before he went to sleep. And at Christmas time, once the tree was decorated downstairs in the sitting room, once they had put up the holly and mistletoe, and once she had made the mince pies, her favourite story was *The Snowman* by Raymond Briggs.

Well, one night, after James had had his *Snowman* story, Grandma said goodnight, hugged him tight and, as usual, told him not to let the bedbugs bite. Bertie came up and jumped on his bed to say goodnight, as he often did, if he could get away with it. When Mum and Dad came up, they shooed Bertie off downstairs, and then kissed James goodnight and snuggled him down. Mum told him to be a good little boy and go to sleep, because Father Christmas only brought the Christmas presents you *really* wanted if you were a good little boy.

The trouble was, James didn't feel like being a good little boy and going to sleep at all. He was far too excited about Christmas. It was coming closer and closer – the next day was Christmas Eve, and then Father Christmas would be coming to see him. He would be hitching up

his team of reindeer to the sleigh, piling it high with presents, and setting off around the world, riding through the skies, the reindeer galloping, the bells jingling, to drop off presents to all the children in every country on earth. Christmas was coming!

And as if that wasn't exciting enough, James kept thinking about the story Grandma had just told him. He loved that story so much and was always sad when it was over. He longed to see snow outside his window; wanted the *Snowman* story to happen again. But every time he looked out there was no snow. There *had* to be snow, he thought, or there could be no snowman.

Time and again he sat up in bed to see if any snow was falling. He went over to the window and pressed his face up against the glass to have a better look, to wish for snow to come.

But all he saw was darkness. In the end he gave up, got back into bed, turned on to his sleeping side and put his thumb in his mouth, as he always did, then closed his eyes and pretended to go to sleep.

Chapter Two

James often found that, if he pretended hard enough and squeezed his eyes tight shut, he could really make things happen. So now, because for Christmas he wanted a mountain bike with big fat tyres – a bright green one like Paul Millard had – he knew he had to pretend to go to sleep like a good little boy, as Mum had told him.

James liked Paul Millard. He had always wanted to be best friends with him. James didn't have a best friend – and he knew why. James stuttered and stammered. He always did whenever he opened his mouth and tried to speak. So at school it was better not to speak, not if he could help it. It was all right at home. For a start, he didn't stammer and stutter so much at home – and anyway, Mum and Dad never teased him. Open his mouth at school, and someone was sure to snigger or mimic him or laugh out loud. He kept quiet; kept himself to himself. It's not easy to make friends if you do that. So James spent most of the time on his own. And that made him sad.

He tried not to think about that. He thought about Paul Millard's bright green mountain bike with big fat tyres instead. It made him happier. James pretended as hard as he could to go to sleep like a good little boy. He really wanted Father Christmas to come and bring him that bike. He pretended so well that he soon pretended himself fast asleep.

★ THE SNOWMAN ★

James didn't know it, but outside, as he slept, the snow *did* begin to fall, silently, silently – on the garden, on the duck pond, on his swing and on his trampoline, on the fields and the hedges and the trees, down on the river and up on the moor. All night the snow came floating down. All night he slept.

★ THE SNOWMAN ★

The moment James opened his eyes he knew
the world was different, but at first he couldn't
work out why. He sat up and looked out of the
window. It wasn't day. It wasn't night. If it was
morning already, it wasn't a morning like any
other. The stars and moon were still up there,
so it must still be night, but it was as bright as
day. *Snow!* It had *snowed!*

Silence lay like a blanket over the house, over the farm. And everywhere it was white. The roof of his dad's shed was white; the seat of the swing, Mum's vegetable garden, Dad's tractor – which he must have forgotten to put away again – were white. All the barns and fields and trees, the distant moors under the moon, all was silent and white.

James was still half asleep and muddle-headed, so it was a few moments before he could take it all in, and a few more before he could even begin to believe his eyes. It looked like snow, but no snow was falling. Could it really be snow? Was this a dream?

There was only one way to find out. He pulled
on some clothes over his pyjamas – his trousers
and the thick red jumper his mum had put out
for him; the one he always wore at Christmas.

Not wanting to wake anyone – he knew he was up too early and that they would send him back to bed if they caught him – he tiptoed out of his bedroom and down the stairs, which seemed to creak more loudly than they had ever creaked before. By the back door he put on his wellies.

Bertie wanted to come with him. He sat there in his basket looking up at him, head on one side, begging to be let out. Any moment now he would start squeaking and whining and then barking.

James crouched down. 'All right, B-Bertie,' he whispered. 'B-but if you c-come with me, not a sound, right? P-promise?'

Bertie licked his lips. It wasn't exactly a promise, James thought, but it was as good as he was going to get.

Chapter Three

James opened the door, and then they were out in it; out in the marvellous moonlit white of it, in the still and silence of it. This was snow all right – proper deep, crunchy snow, the real thing, snow like neither James nor Bertie had ever seen before. Bertie ran off at once to explore, following his nose as he always did, wagging his tail wildly – but, to James's great relief, not barking. The snow seemed to have silenced Bertie too.

★ THE SNOWMAN ★

James trudged off through the snow, down past the weedy duck pond towards the bottom of the garden, and opened the gate out into Oak Tree Field beyond. Here he was far enough from the house not to be seen. Now he could do as he pleased – jump up and down in the snow, roll down the hill in it, cavort and somersault and frolic in it. Bertie did the same.

★ THE SNOWMAN ★

James swung on the oak tree's lowest branch, and the snow fell down the back of his neck. He stomped round the tree in a great wide circle, leaving deep footprints behind him in the snow. Breathless with the fun of it, he stood there looking all around, admiring the circle of footprints he had made.

That was when a sudden brilliant thought came into his head. He knew at once what he was going to do, and how he was going to do it.

All thoughts of Christmas, and presents, and Father Christmas – even thoughts of the bright green mountain bike – had vanished. Nothing mattered to James now but the snow, and the huge snowman he had just decided he was going to make. Now, right now.

He began by making a snowball, just a small one, but squeezed tight in his hands till it was hard. Then he got down on his knees in the snow and began to roll it along – slowly at first – into a bigger one, which became an even bigger one, as big as a football now. Even this was not quite big enough, he thought; not yet. So he rolled it and rolled it, until it was the perfect size for what he had in mind.

★ THE SNOWMAN ★

Bertie came leaping across the field, tongue hanging out, tail whirling. 'Watch, B-Bertie,' James told him. 'Sit and watch.'

So Bertie sat and watched as James finished his giant snowball and began to build a huge tower of snow, packing it higher and higher, till it was above his head, as high as he could reach.

Then he was trimming and patting down the sides so that it was just right. But now he had a problem. It was *too* tall, *too* high. Bertie was looking up at him, head on one side as if to say: *Now what are you going to do, clever clogs? You need a ladder, don't you?*

James ran back to his dad's shed and fetched the stepladder. Putting a ladder up in the snow isn't easy because it keeps sinking when you stand on it. But James managed. Climbing it wasn't easy either, especially when carrying a huge snowball. But after a wobble or two James managed to do that as well.

Gently, carefully, he lowered the snowball

into place, and began packing snow round it so that it stayed there and didn't fall off. That done, he climbed down the ladder again, and stood back to look up and admire his snowman, who now had a proper head. He wasn't finished, but he was already brilliant; the biggest and best snowman James had ever seen!

Bertie must have thought he was some kind of a giant, because he suddenly began barking his head off, and wouldn't stop. He ran round and round the snowman, yelping and yapping in wild excitement. James ran after him, trying to catch him, to calm him down.

But Bertie wasn't going to be caught. He was telling this huge white giant of a stranger just what he thought of him, as loudly as he could. From the stables, Big was neighing, Little was braying. The ducks were quacking from the pond, the sheep bleating from the barn, and soon the pigs and cows were joining in. It was a whole animal chorus! The lights went on in the farmhouse.

'Oh, thanks a lot, B-Bertie,' James said. 'Look what you've started. You've woken everyone up, M-Mum, Dad *and* Grandma.'

So of course it wasn't long before Dad came running out into the field. 'What's going on? What's all the racket about? What are you doing out here, James?' he said, and he sounded really cross. But then he noticed the snowman. 'Wow! What a wonderful snowman! You built that?'

'All b-by m-myself,' James said proudly.

'Well, he's a great snowman,' Dad said proudly too. 'But if you ask me, he needs eyes and a nose and a mouth. And a hat. You can have my old hat, if you like. It's in the shed. Come along.'

He didn't seem at all cross any more.

He took James's hand and walked him back through the snow. 'Mum's a bit upset, you know; so's Grandma. All that terrible racket and hullabaloo from the farmyard. Quite a noise the animals made – woke us all up. Then we discovered you weren't in your bed, and we looked everywhere for you. But I wasn't that worried. One glance out of the window and I knew you'd be out in the snow. I was a boy once, you know. But I never built such a magnificent snowman. Massive, he is; taller than I am.'

'You won't t-tell anyone about m-my snowman, will you, Dad? N-not until he's finished. I want him to b-be a surprise.'

Chapter Four

Dad didn't say a word. At breakfast he just smiled a few secret smiles at James across the kitchen table; just winked a few winks. James had never eaten breakfast so fast in all his life. He never said a word – he was too busy eating, and while he was eating, he was working out what he would need to finish building his snowman.

He gobbled down his cereal, gulped down his milk, wolfed down his toast, giving the crusts sneakily to Bertie under the table, because when Grandma came to stay, she always made him eat his crusts, which he didn't like at all. Besides, giving them to Bertie helped him finish up his breakfast even faster.

'Finished!' he said. And he was off.

'Don't forget to wrap up warm,' Grandma said. 'Your nice green scarf – the one I knitted for you – and your woolly gloves, and make sure you put on your thick socks inside those wellies.'

'And don't forget my old hat. It's in the shed,' Dad called out after him. 'Got to keep warm out there.'

James knew well enough who he was talking about, who the hat was for, but no one else did.

He loved having secrets with his dad. He was glad Dad had reminded him about the old hat. He'd forgotten all about it. He did put on the green scarf, but he didn't bother with anything else.

On his way out, James went to the larder and found everything he thought he would need for his snowman: a tangerine, some apples, and a handful of those horrible Brussels sprouts that only Grandma liked. Then he picked up a couple of pieces of coal from the coal shed. These were all just perfect for what James had in mind.

So, his pockets stuffed with fruit and vegetables and coal, James stomped out across the garden, fetched Dad's old hat from the shed, and then went out into the field. Bertie ran on ahead of him, and was already prowling round the giant snowman, growling.

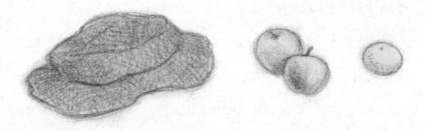

'It's all right, B-Bertie,' James told him. 'He won't hurt you. I know he looks a b-bit strange at the m-moment. But you just watch. I'm g-going to m-make him the happiest, friendliest snowman ever. Watch.'

So Bertie sat and watched as James climbed up to the very top of the ladder. He had to, so that he could reach. The ladder wobbled a bit, but James didn't mind. He took off his dad's hat and put it on the snowman's head. It fitted perfectly.

He had two nice little apples for the ears. They looked just the right shape – ear-shaped. James

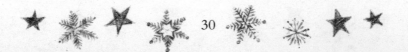

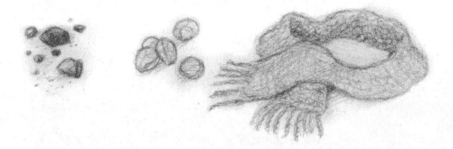

pushed them in quite deep so that they stayed there, and then he pulled the hat down low like his dad did, so you couldn't see them any more. That way they would be warm. 'With those ears the snowman will b-be able t-to understand everything we're saying, B-Bertie. You'll see,' said James.

By now he could hardly feel his fingers or his feet, but he didn't mind. There was still so much to do. 'N-nose,' he told Bertie, taking the tangerine out of his coat pocket and showing him. 'It's g-got to b-be an orange n-nose, because

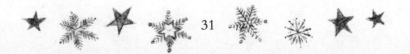

orange is m-my favourite c-colour.' He stuck it in as hard as he could. Now the snowman had his own bright orange nose, which suited him perfectly. 'There. That won't fall off, will it? And look, it's a lovely n-nose. He'll b-be able to smell with it, won't he? You c-can't live without a n-nose, can you, B-Bertie?'

Bertie swished his tail in the snow and yawned and licked his lips, which he often did when he agreed.

'N-now, he's g-got to have eyes so he c-can see us,' James said, taking the two pieces of coal out of his pocket. 'Look, B-Bertie, he's g-going to have b-black eyes, smiling b-black eyes. He'll b-be happy with those, won't he?'

But the snowman's face didn't look happy. 'Maybe he's c-cold,' said James. 'You can't b-be happy if you're c-cold, c-can you, B-Bertie? He hasn't got m-many clothes on, has he?'

And that gave him another brilliant idea. He took off his green scarf – the one Grandma had knitted for him – reached out and tied it round the snowman's neck. He looked a little warmer perhaps, but he still didn't seem much happier.

James got down off the ladder, stood back and looked up at his snowman. Bertie looked up at him too. Dad's old hat was keeping his head warm, and the scarf suited him fine. It looked grand on him, blowing in the wind, but James could now see that a scarf on its own wouldn't keep him really warm.

'He n-needs a c-coat, B-Bertie,' James said. 'But he's far too b-big for any c-coat we've got at home – even Dad's. I m-mean, we don't know any giants, do we? But m-maybe, m-maybe, if I g-gave him a pretend c-coat, so that it looked really real and he felt it was really real, then m-maybe that would k-keep him p-properly warm and m-make him happy. What do you think, B-Bertie?'

Bertie put his head on one side, as if to say – and he talked really well with his eyes – *I think a coat is just what that snowman needs, but it must have buttons, so he can do it up. Lots of buttons. You've still got Grandma's horrible Brussels sprouts in your pocket, haven't you? They'd do fine as buttons. A lot better than eating them, that's for sure.*

'You're a genius d-dog, B-Bertie,' James said, crouching down to give him a cuddle. Then up the ladder he went again. He took all the Brussels sprouts out of his pocket and, starting at the top near the snowman's neck, came slowly down the ladder, giving his snowman Brussels-sprout button after Brussels-sprout button till he had

none left. In the end the snowman's coat had five buttons from top to bottom, all of them as green as Brussels sprouts.

Chapter Five

But even with his new buttoned-up coat, the snowman still didn't look happy. That was when James heard his dad singing away in the milking parlour. And that was when he remembered something Mum sang to him sometimes – Mum and Dad both liked singing it – if ever he was feeling a bit sad and miserable, as he was quite often on his way to school in the mornings. She'd put her arm round him, wipe away his tears and sing that song about when you are smiling and the world smiles with you. He liked her singing that song. It always cheered him up – for a while at least.

'That's it, B-Bertie!' he cried, climbing the ladder again. 'He n-needs a smile – the snowman n-needs a smile, because smiling m-makes you happy; m-makes the whole world happy.'

A smile would be easy enough to make, he thought. And with his finger he drew a smile across the snowman's face – a huge wide curve of a smile; a happy smile!

Bertie liked what he saw. He was barking – not wildly but happily, his tail whirling. Then he started chasing it round and round, which he only did when he was especially happy.

James climbed down the ladder, then stood back and looked up at his snowman. He liked

what he saw too. With that smile on his face, his
snowman was happy at last. So James smiled too,
and hummed his mum's song.

As he looked up at him, James decided that he loved his happy snowman more than anything – even more than Bertie (but he wasn't going to tell him that), and far more than a bright green mountain bike with big fat tyres (but all the same he still hoped he'd get one for Christmas).

There was so much to do that day – there always was on Christmas Eve. James kept asking Mum and Dad and Grandma to come out and see his surprise. He was longing to show everyone his snowman now that he was finished. But everyone was too busy.

Grandma was busy mixing the chestnut stuffing for the turkey, and she had to get the Brussels sprouts ready too. So she couldn't come and look.

Mum was busy giving the sheep their hay, and feeding the hens and collecting the eggs, and taking Big and Little out to their field. So she couldn't come and look.

And Dad was busy with the cows and calves and pigs, and he said he'd already seen the snowman, but he'd come as soon as he could. But he didn't come and look either.

So that afternoon, feeling a bit sad, James took Bertie out to Oak Tree Field, where his snowman stood waiting for him. James said hello, and told him why his family couldn't come and meet him yet – they would later, he said, when they weren't so busy.

As he talked, he patted down the snow where it had fallen away a bit, and tried to put back all the Brussels-sprout buttons that had fallen off – but only three would stay in. James hoped that would be enough to keep his coat on.

Then he went sliding down the hill on his bottom to show the snowman how fast he could go. That soon cheered him up. And the snowman seemed to like it too. James even thought he heard him laughing once – a deep booming laugh; a jolly laugh, like no one else's.

James needed to talk to his snowman – he wanted to get to know him better. So he rolled himself another big snowball, made it flat on top, and then sat down on it right in front of the snowman. Sitting there on his snow chair, James told the snowman all about himself – well, not all; just the interesting things, like his best toys and Paul Millard, who he wanted as his best friend, and the green mountain bike, and how he wished, wished, wished he could stop stuttering and stammering, because everyone at school laughed at him. And then he told him that his favourite food was raspberry jelly, and that he hated Brussels sprouts.

The snowman smiled and listened quite happily. So that cheered James up. Something else was cheering him up too, but he couldn't think what it was. Though he still felt a little sad that everyone was too busy to come and look at his surprise snowman.

Chapter Six

He was just telling the snowman how much he wanted a green mountain bike like Paul Millard's for Christmas when he heard the sound of footsteps crunching in the snow behind him. He turned round. They were all there – Mum, Dad and Grandma.

'We've come to see your surprise,' said Dad.

'Wow! Wow! Wow!' said Mum, gazing up at the snowman in wonder. 'Amazing! And the best thing about him is his smile.'

'He's magnificent, James,' said Grandma, reaching out to touch the snowman. 'He's wonderful, almost like he's real – like he's living and breathing. I love those three lovely coat buttons too. Do you know, I *thought* I was missing a few Brussels sprouts! Still, on cold days like this, you've got to keep yourself buttoned up, even if you're a snowman.'

James skipped through the snow all the way back to the house. He was so happy that they all loved his snowman as much as he did. He fell over a few times because it's not easy to skip in the snow. They all laughed at that, and Bertie joined in, barking his head off, and then he

chased his tail again. So they all laughed some more.

Their laughter echoed out over the fields around them. Big and Little neighed and brayed from their field, and soon all the animals seemed to be joining in. The whole farm rang with laughter. And James was sure he could hear his snowman laughing too – a deep booming laugh; a jolly laugh, like no one else's.

James wanted to spend the whole afternoon with his snowman out in Oak Tree Field, but they wouldn't let him. 'You were out there all morning, James,' said Mum.

'It's bitter out there,' said Grandma. 'You'll catch a cold. You stay in the warm and help your grandma. There's plenty to do. You could start by fetching in the logs for the fire.'

'Don't you worry,' said Dad, already laughing

– with Dad you could always tell when a joke was coming – 'your snowman will be fine out there. It doesn't matter much if a snowman gets cold, does it?'

He pestered them and pestered them, so in the end they let him go out again, just before dark, to say goodnight to his snowman. He looked very lonely standing out there all on his own.

'Sleep well, Mr Snowman,' James said, looking up at him. 'I'll dream about you, and you dream about me, then you won't be lonely, will you? Christmas Day tomorrow. Father Christmas might bring me my bright green mountain bike. That's if I'm a good little boy, Mum says. Then we could go for a ride on it together, couldn't we? Got to go. Don't want to, but it's my teatime, and I promised Mum I'd be back inside before she could count to five hundred.'

And James walked through the snow back to the house, feeling on top of the world.

That night it was Mum's turn to read him a story. James said he wanted *The Snowman*, but Mum said he always wanted that one, and he had a snowman of his own now, which was a lot better than a story about one. And anyway she wanted to read him her favourite Christmas story, which was *The Night Before Christmas*. It was quite good, but not as good as *The Snowman*. But he didn't tell Mum that.

Afterwards Dad and Grandma came up, and he had more hugs. As usual, Grandma told him not to let the bedbugs bite, and Dad said he mustn't try to stay awake to see Father Christmas come creeping into his room with all the presents to fill up his stocking.

Dad laid out the stocking on the end of James's bed. 'It's empty now,' he said, 'but you go to sleep like a good little boy, and when you wake up it'll be full of presents. You'll see.'

And then they were all gone and James was alone. He hated being alone at school. He was alone in his bedroom now, but that was all right. Somehow he never felt alone at home, not in the same way. He thought of his snowman, alone in his field. The owl hooted. *Oowit, oowit, oowit. They don't go* too-wit too-woo *at all,* James thought. *And that owl is alone too. And he stutters and stammers as well. Maybe that's why I like owls.*

But then he thought, *None of us is alone, not really. Sometimes we think we are, but I know the owl is out there and I know the snowman is out there. And there are voices downstairs. So I'm not alone anyway, not really.*

James liked thinking. Thinking and dreaming were his two favourite things.

Chapter Seven

Downstairs the clock in the hallway was chiming out the hours, and James was still awake every hour it happened. He heard everyone coming upstairs to bed, creakily – Mum and Dad together, then Grandma. And still the owl hooted, still the clock chimed out the hours. James wasn't thinking about Father Christmas coming; he could think only of his snowman, and he had the strangest feeling that his snowman was thinking of him.

He got out of bed and went to his window. It was a bright night, a white night. Under the moon and the stars he could just see the big tree in Oak Tree Field. He could hear the owl hooting. And he thought he could just make out his snowman, with Dad's old hat on top.

'G'night, Mr Snowman,' he whispered. 'See you in the morning.'

Back in his bed, he snuggled down. He still couldn't stop thinking about his snowman. Outside, the owl hooted again. Downstairs, the clock chimed again. *Morning will come faster if I go to sleep,* James thought. *Then it'll be Christmas Day, and I'll wake up, and Father Christmas will have filled my stocking and brought my bright green mountain bike with the big fat tyres. And, best of all, I'll be able to go out and be with my snowman again. Grandma was right. He is magnificent; he is wonderful.* James closed his eyes and pretended to sleep; pretended hard – so hard that very soon he drifted off and was lost in his dreams.

It was still the middle of the night when he woke. He sat up and looked out of the window. There was the big oak tree out in the field, and there was his snowman. And then, and then – and James didn't believe it at first, and you're not going to believe it either – the snowman was waving to him; yes, *waving* to him! James rubbed his eyes and looked again. It was true. The snowman was waving, beckoning to him. He wanted James to come down and see him.

James was out of bed as quick as he could, lickety-split, dressing gown on, slippers on. Soon he was tiptoeing past Grandma's room, down the creaky stairs, and towards the front door. And, still tiptoeing so as not to wake Bertie, he was opening the door and running out across the snow – in his slippers. He hadn't even stopped to put on his wellies!

He ran through the gate into Oak Tree Field, and there was the big tree, every branch and twig still covered in snow. But where was his snowman? He was nowhere to be seen! He had gone.

And then from behind the tree came a waving arm, then a kicking leg, then a head – his snowman's head, the face still smiling, and still wearing Dad's old hat. Now the snowman was walking; walking across the field towards him! Now he was shaking James by the hand.

'All night I've been standing there and thinking,' said the snowman, and his voice sounded so jolly and booming and deep. 'I was thinking what it might be like inside your house. I've never been in a house before.'

'Well, why don't you come in then, Mr Snowman?' James said. 'I'll show you around. But I'm not sure you'll fit through the door. You're so big. And we mustn't make any noise, or else we'll wake everyone up, and Grandma hates being woken up at night. It makes her proper grumpy.'

The snowman took his hand, and off they ran together over the frozen snow, across the garden, past the swing and the trampoline

towards the house, the owl flying above them on silent wings. The snowman had to breathe in very deep to get through the door. But he managed it, just.

James showed him into the sitting room first. Bertie was fast asleep on the sofa, where he shouldn't have been. The last thing James wanted was for the dog to wake up. He put a finger to his lips, and the snowman did the same. They understood one another perfectly.

And how the snowman loved the Christmas tree – all the glittering dingly-danglies, and especially the silver star on the top and the little Father Christmas underneath the tree; the one Grandma loved so much because she had had the same Father Christmas under her Christmas tree every year when she was little.

The snowman was trying to sit down on a

chair. He tried Grandma's chair. Too small. He tried Mum's chair. Too small. The only one big enough was the chair by the fire, where Dad often sat when he took off his socks and wiggled his toes – which Grandma didn't like at all. The snowman sat back in the chair just like Dad did, but he didn't take off his socks or wiggle his toes because he didn't have any socks to take off or any toes to wiggle.

But suddenly the snowman was not looking happy at all. He jumped up and backed away from the fire. James saw at once what was upsetting him. It was the heat of the fire! It was too much for the snowman. It was warming him up, and he didn't like it one bit. He liked being cold. He *had* to be cold.

So James took him into the kitchen and opened up the lid of the freezer. It was just about long enough for his snowman. 'Lie down in that for a bit, Mr Snowman,' he said. 'You'll feel a lot cooler, a lot better.'

So the snowman lay back and snuggled down happily on his frozen bed made of bags of frozen peas and frozen broad beans and frozen apples and frozen blackcurrants and frozen gooseberries – everything Mum had gathered in from the garden during the summer.

Chapter Eight

Once the snowman was feeling cold enough again, he was clambering out of the freezer, ready to explore the rest of the house. James took him upstairs, creakily, into his bedroom and showed him all his toys. They sat down and played with James's train set, and James introduced him to every single one of his cuddly animals. The snowman liked his polar bear best.

They even crept into Grandma's room. Luckily she was sleeping soundly, and snoring quite loudly, as she did sometimes. By her bed was a photograph of James, who the snowman recognized at once.

In the bathroom James showed him how he brushed his teeth. The snowman wanted to smell everything on the shelf – the shampoo, Grandma's special lavender soap, which she didn't like anyone else using, and the talcum powder. James showed him how to shake the powder out. He shouldn't have done that because, before he knew it, the snowman was going wild with the talcum powder, shaking it all over the bathroom, all over himself and all over James too!

After that James got him out of the house as quickly as he could before any other disasters could happen. The whole house smelled of talcum powder!

They ran out into the garden. The snowman took one look at the swing and wanted to have a go, but he was too big to fit on it. So James sat on it and the snowman pushed him. Higher and higher he went – so high that James felt he was almost flying.

Then, suddenly, the snowman wasn't pushing any more. He was running towards the trampoline and climbing on. After only one bounce he just seemed to love it. James ran over and climbed on as well. They held hands, and bounced and bounced and bounced. James had never bounced so high in his life. This was the best fun he had ever had. In the end they had to stop because they were laughing so much.

Maybe it was their laughter that woke up Big

and Little. They began neighing and braying from their stables. The snowman wanted to find out who was making all that noise. He took James's hand, and off they ran to the stables.

Big and Little were only too pleased to see them. No one usually came to see them in the middle of the night! Though they thought it was rather strange when they were led out into the snowy field, and they thought it stranger still when James got up on Little and the snowman got up on Big. But they didn't mind, not one bit. Nights in the stables could be long and boring. Off they trotted, and then away they galloped through the snow. It was all James could do to hang on.

Up in the big oak tree the owl was watching everything, too amazed even to hoot. The snowman rode Big as if he had been riding all

his life. Big and Little had never galloped so fast before, and they had never had so much fun. They were soon completely puffed out. And, by the time they took them back to their stables, so were James and the snowman.

That was when the snowman saw Dad's tractor. He walked round and round it, chuckling all the time, his smile becoming broader and broader. He swept the snow off the seat, climbed up and sat on it. 'Well?' he said with a twinkle in his eye. 'How does this thing work? Are you coming or not?'

James wasn't going to miss this. Up he climbed and sat on the snowman's lap, just like he did with Dad. He showed him where the key was – Dad always left it in. He showed him the gears and the steering wheel and the throttle.

That's all the snowman needed. With a turn of

the key the engine started up. With a grinding of the gears and a push on the throttle the tractor began to move – slowly at first, jerkily, but soon they were out in Oak Tree Field and roaring along, bouncing along. Round and round the tree they went. Up on his branch, the owl was getting giddy watching them. Round and round his head went.

Down the hill they roared, and along the river. They scared the deer in the woods, woke up the badgers and foxes, and then came thundering up the hill again, back into Oak Tree Field. The snowman drove that tractor like a proper farmer, as if he'd been doing it all his life. He chortled and chuckled and laughed out loud. He loved every moment of it. So did James. He never wanted the ride to end!

Chapter Nine

Afterwards, as they walked back through the garden together, James thought that all the fun and games must be over. He couldn't have been more wrong.

The snowman took his hand. 'I've had such a good time, James,' he told him. 'This home of yours is full of nice surprises. Would you like to see *mine*? I haven't got a farm, but I have got a bit of a surprise to show you.'

And at that moment the snowman began to run – slowly at first, but then faster and faster and faster. He had long legs and James had short legs, so with every step James was finding it harder and harder to keep up.

But suddenly he didn't have to run any more because he couldn't – his feet weren't touching the ground! They were going so fast they were taking off. His legs were running through thin air! They were flying! The snowman had his arm round him, and they were *flying*!

James looked down. There was his house with the smoke coming out of the chimney; there was the farm, there were the barns, there was his swing, there was Dad's shed, there was his trampoline. But they were all getting smaller and smaller.

Higher and higher they flew, over the fields

and the woods and the river, out over the moor. Above them the moon and the stars; below them a world of white.

James looked round and saw that they weren't alone! There were other snowmen flying along behind – dozens of them; hundreds of them! But none of the others had a boy flying with him. He was the only one, and James liked that. He had never felt more special in his life.

James looked ahead. 'Where are we going?' he cried.

But the snowman only laughed his booming jolly laugh, so James wasn't worried. He was enjoying himself too much to be worried. Ahead, on the horizon, the sky was aglow. As they flew on, he could see the glittering lights of a big city, with tall towers, wide roads, and a dark river running through it; over the

bridges the cars came and went.

James looked up. Stars filled the sky as far as he could see. He loved stars; his dad loved them too – he knew some of their names, and so did James. But he had never been as close to them as this. Up there was the Plough and the Big Dipper, and the Milky Way was everywhere.

When he looked down again, the brightness of the city was gone. There were no lights to be seen any more; no houses, no fields, no snowy whiteness; only a darkness that shone in the moonlight, a darkness that James knew was the darkness of the sea.

Down they flew, lower and lower, over little waves, huge waves, and then over little icebergs, huge icebergs.

The snowman was pointing ahead. 'Look, James,' he said. 'Home. My home.'

It was a land made entirely of snow. Below them now there were no more trees or fields or rivers or houses, no more glowing lights, no cars or bright city buildings, just snow. And it was all so empty, so beautiful, so quiet. Over white mountains they floated high, and along white valleys they flew low over the snow, the snowman's arm round James, still holding him tight.

'Almost there now,' said the snowman. 'I'm not very good at landing, James, I'm afraid. I never really got the hang of it. But don't you worry. There's plenty of snow about, and it's always deep. We'll have a nice soft landing, you'll see.'

But, as they neared the ground, it seemed to James that they were flying over it faster and faster, not slower and slower. So, despite what the snowman had said, he was beginning to be worried; very worried indeed. But, when they did land, although they bumped and bounced and slid along in the snow for quite a while, and rolled over and over in it, they ended up safe and sound, because the snow, as the snowman had said, was softer than the deepest cushion.

The snowman was there to help James to his feet. 'Here we are, James,' he said. 'Snowmen's land. Our home. This is where we all come back to, where we snowmen all belong. We can't stay long in your world. We have to live where it's cold. And we aren't alone. Look up there!'

Chapter Ten

James looked up, and saw then that all down the valley snowmen were landing. Like his snowman, most of them weren't very good at it. They bumped and bounced and rolled and tumbled and somersaulted in the snow. But in the end they all helped one another to their feet, exchanging greetings, laughing out loud; all of them, James could see, happy to be home.

'I hope you enjoyed your flight,' said the

snowman, taking James's hand in his. 'Now come along with me. There's a very special someone I want you to meet.'

As they tramped through the snow, the other snowmen joined them, and they all wanted to welcome James, to say hello. He had a lot of 'hellos' to say, but he didn't mind because they were all so friendly.

His snowman seemed only too proud to introduce him to everyone as 'my good friend James'. James loved that. They were words that warmed his heart. And that was just as well, because by now that was the only part of him that was warm at all.

On they tramped, deeper and deeper into the valley, until they found themselves walking into a huge cave of snow and ice, where hundreds of other snowmen were waiting for them. The cave was full of jolly chatter and deep laughter, and there was music playing. There was singing and dancing. It was a party! A snowmen's party.

But, as they came in, as they were noticed, the music stopped. The dancing and the singing stopped, and the snowmen were all smiling at James, making way for him, and then they were clapping him.

His snowman squeezed his hand. 'My family,

they all like you, James,' he said. 'I knew they would.'

'You've got a very, very, very big family, Mr Snowman,' James said, slightly nervous at all the attention, kind though it was.

Each of the snowmen, he noticed, was dressed differently. None had a hat like Dad's old hat. And none, so far as he could see, had three green Brussels-sprout buttons on his coat. There were quite a few with tangerine noses, but more with carrot noses, which didn't look nearly as good. None, James thought, had a scarf as bright and beautiful as his snowman's green scarf; the one Grandma had knitted.

James was full of questions, and there was one in particular. 'Mr Snowman,' he asked, 'who's this very special someone you said you wanted me to meet?'

'Right there,' replied his snowman. 'Look.'

And just as he was speaking, through the crowd of snowmen came someone much smaller and redder and chubbier than any of them, with the longest, whitest beard James had ever seen. He looked just like Grandma's Father Christmas they always had underneath the Christmas tree at home – except bigger; a lot, lot, lot bigger. And this Father Christmas walked and talked.

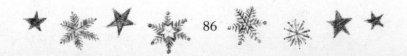

'Welcome to the North Pole. Welcome to our world, James,' he said, coming towards him, smiling as broadly as all the snowmen.

Father Christmas? Was this really Father Christmas talking to him? Was he living and breathing? Was he shaking him by the hand? Was this all happening?

'Hello, you!' Father Christmas said. 'I was coming to see you tonight. And now *you've* come to see *me*. You're James, aren't you? And you live on a farm with your mum and dad, and Grandma comes for Christmas, doesn't she? Address – let me think . . . Oh yes: Paradise Farm, Iddesleigh, EX19 8SN, and that's in Devon, am I right? And that's in England. And you've got the dog that doesn't like me coming down your chimney and disturbing him. Growly dog. Nice chimney, though. Big and wide and warm. A bit

sooty, but then it would be. It's a chimney.'

James was speechless. Father Christmas knew everything about him! His name, his address – he even knew about Bertie!

'You've come just in time for the party, James,' Father Christmas went on. 'I always have a bit of a do before visiting children all over the world. Busy night ahead. And I've been busy with all those presents. You know the bit I hate? Wrapping them. I mean, I have to wrap presents for all the children everywhere. And that's a lot! Still, I mustn't complain – I have a little help from my snowman friends. But have you ever tried wrapping a bright green mountain bike with big fat tyres?' He was shaking his head. 'The things some children ask for – I don't know!'

Chapter Eleven

Father Christmas was chuckling as he put an arm round James's shoulder and led him over to a huge ice table covered with food and drinks. There were mostly ice creams and ice lollies, but James was happy with that, and so, by the looks of it, were all the snowmen. There was chocolate-chip ice cream, there was caramel, there was strawberry, all of them James's favourites.

They pulled crackers, they sang songs, and then the fun and jollification really began.

There was a live band: one snowman on the drums, another five or six on fiddles, two or three on flutes and whistles, another on the saxophone – and he was brilliant – and Father Christmas himself on the squeeze box. It was a great sound, and they all had a great knees-up – as James's grandma would have called it.

They danced lots of Scottish dances – quite a few of the snowmen came from Scotland because it's often very snowy up there, James was told. There were reels and jigs and all sorts, and James danced every one of them with his snowman. All night long they danced and danced, up and down and round about. They had a ball! They had the best knees-up, the best fun, the best jollification ever.

And then a marvellous and beautiful and quite unexpected thing happened. Well, come to think of it, most of James's adventures with the snowman had been quite unexpected. One of the snowmen came running into the cave, waving his hands for all the music and dancing to stop. When the cave had fallen quite silent, he started speaking.

'It's time. It's happening,' said the snowman. 'Come – come quickly! The lights – the Northern Lights!'

And they all ran out at once, James clinging to his snowman's hand so he didn't get knocked over in the stampede of excited snowmen.

There they all stood, every one of them hushed and gazing up into the sky. James wondered for a moment what they were all looking at. But then he saw it for himself. The sky on the horizon was changing colour before his very eyes! And the colours were moving, weaving, wafting in and out of one another, making rippling waves of blue and green and yellow and violet and pink and orange and white and red. James had seen rainbows back at home – even a double rainbow once – but never anything like this.

'The Northern Lights,' his snowman whispered. 'Aurora Borealis. Isn't it the most wondrous sight? It always happens on the night before Christmas. And it means the time has come.'

'The time for what, Mr Snowman?' James asked him. James couldn't understand it, but every time he spoke to the snowman he felt on top of the world.

'You'll soon see,' the snowman replied. 'It won't be long now. Keep looking or you might miss them. You'll hear them before you see them. Listen.'

And, as James listened, he heard the sound of bells – jingling bells coming from inside the cave – and in among the jingling bells came a voice he recognized; the voice of Father Christmas. 'Giddy up, my beauties!' he was calling. 'Giddy up! We've got a long, long way to go, and a lot of children to visit all over the world. So giddy up, my beauties! Jingle those bells.'

And as James and the snowmen watched, they saw a team of reindeer pulling a sleigh carrying Father Christmas, a mountain of presents piled high behind him. Everyone stood back to let them pass as they came trotting by. The snowmen were all clapping and cheering and singing them on their way. James did too, his heart full of happiness.

Chapter Twelve

As the sleigh swished past, Father Christmas
waved at everyone, and James was sure he saw
him give a great big wink, specially for him.
Maybe with that wink, he thought, *he's trying to
tell me that he's bringing me a bright green mountain
bike with big fat tyres, just like Paul Millard's; that
it's on the back of his sleigh, and it's on its way to my
house right now.*

But try as he might, James couldn't see anything that looked like a wrapped-up mountain bike in among all the presents piled high on the sleigh. But maybe it was there, he thought, hidden away under all the others. He closed his eyes and hoped so hard that it was.

And with another 'Giddy up, my beauties! Jingle those bells!' from Father Christmas, the reindeer were galloping, galloping, and the sleigh was swishing, swishing, louder, louder through the snow.

Then they were galloping through the air, rising into the sky, up and up, faster, faster, smaller, smaller, into the wonderful Northern Lights; in and out of the yellow, the red, the white, the violet, the green, and disappearing at last into the blue and the pink.

And still James could hear the jingling bells. *Those bells*, he thought, *will be heard by children all over the globe* – bells he would listen out for when he got home to bed, unless Father Christmas came before he got back. He hoped he would be home in time. To see Father Christmas leave the North Pole, and then to see him arrive at his home with the reindeer and the sleigh and all the jingling bells – imagine that! That would

really be something! He had to get home fast.

'Well, James,' said his snowman, 'I'd better get you home, hadn't I?' It was as if he could read James's mind. 'The party's over for another year. Did you enjoy it as much as I did; as much as we *all* did?'

'More than you,' said James, 'more than anyone.' And he meant it. Again, as he was speaking, he suddenly felt on top of the

world, and he still didn't know why.

But then, as he looked around, he began to feel sad. The glorious lights were gone, the jingling bells with them. All the snowmen were hugging each other, saying fond goodbyes, and one by one, two by two, they took off, flying away, arms outstretched like wings, singing to one another a song of farewell as they did so.

James's snowman said his goodbyes to his friends, and one by one they gave James a hug too. James loved that, except that being hugged by lots of snowmen was quite cold. But all the hugging was over soon enough.

'Home, James?' said his snowman, taking his hand. 'Hold on tight now.'

And up and away they soared, over the silence of a wide white wilderness, along snow-covered valleys, over white peaks of mountains. Homeward bound, homeward.

Out over the dark shining sea, dotted below with huge icebergs and little icebergs, and now there was the glow of a great city ahead, and the bright lights of buildings and the moving lights of cars.

Soon enough they were clear of the city. Above them now were the moon and the stars, a whole sky full of them. And down below there were fields and woods and farms and houses and villages, all covered in white. Then James saw that they were his fields, his farm, his house. There was Oak Tree Field just below them.

'Remember, James,' said his snowman, 'I'm not very good at this landing lark! Hang on!'

James had already remembered. He hung on tight, closed his eyes and waited for the bumpy landing. It was even bumpier and bouncier than

★ THE SNOWMAN ★

before. They somersaulted over and over before they finally slid to a slithering stop right under the oak tree.

Above them, the owl woke up and hooted at them. He was not a happy owl at all. He didn't like being woken up, not one bit, and he was telling them so. He hooted at them again and again.

Chapter Thirteen

It was the owl that woke Grandma. She lay there for a while trying to go back to sleep, but the owl went on hooting, and the moon was shining brightly through her window. She just couldn't get back to sleep. So in the end she got out of bed and went over to the window, hoping at least to see this noisy owl, because Grandma loved owls. And, sure enough, she did see the owl flying round and round the oak tree. But she saw something else too.

She saw James out there in the snow in the middle of the moonlit night, out there in his dressing gown and slippers. She was about to open the window and tell him to come in at once before he caught his death of cold when she saw something else – or, rather, someone else – with him; it was the snowman, the magnificent snowman James had made.

To begin with Grandma thought that James was just standing there looking up at his snowman; that he had gone out there in the middle of the night to make sure he was all right. And she thought that was a kind and loving thing to do. If she called him in, then that might wake his mum and dad, and then James would get into trouble for being outside at night in the snow, in just his dressing gown and slippers. So she stood there at the window and watched.

★ THE SNOWMAN ★

And what did Grandma see? She saw the snowman move. She saw the snowman walking with his arm round James, away from the oak tree and down towards the gate into the garden.

This must be a dream, she thought. *I must still be asleep. I never remember my dreams, but I really hope I remember this one.*

Then, as she watched, and to her complete and utter amazement, the two of them started to dance. They were dancing, dancing in the snow! They were doing a jig together! She pinched herself hard to wake up, and then she knew that she had to believe her eyes, that she was already awake.

But still she had to make quite sure. She pulled on her dressing gown over her jimjams, and went softly, softly down the stairs. Putting on her wellies by the door, she stepped out into the cold moonlit night.

James and the snowman were still dancing, and enjoying it so much that they didn't see Grandma coming towards them across the garden. The snowman turned and saw her first, and stopped dancing. For a few moments James went on dancing on his own. Then he saw Grandma too. He didn't know what to say; nor did Grandma, nor did the snowman.

Grandma spoke first. 'Did I just see what I thought I saw?' she asked them. They nodded. 'Have you been out here long, James?'

'Quite long, Grandma,' he told her, finding his voice at last. 'Long enough for Mr Snowman to fly me all the way to the North Pole and back; long enough to meet all his snowmen friends and have an ice-cream party and a knees-up with them – oh yes, and with Father Christmas too.'

That was the moment James knew why he felt so happy, so on top of the world. He was only stuttering a little now – sometimes hardly at all. The words were flowing out of him, not tripping over one another as they usually did. It was as if he wasn't doing the talking at all; as if all the words were speaking themselves!

Chapter Fourteen

With scarcely a pause for breath James told his grandma everything that had happened: about Father Christmas's sleigh, and the reindeer and the jingling bells, and the Northern Lights flickering across the sky, and how the snowman had flown him all the way there and back, high over mountains and cities and low over sea and waves and icebergs, and how he'd had the best time of his life.

'He flew you?' Grandma said. 'What, up there in the sky? All the way there and back?'

James nodded. The snowman nodded. The owl hooted from the oak tree.

'James?' said Grandma, utterly and completely amazed and astonished. 'You're not stuttering any more – d'you realize that?'

'I know, Grandma,' James replied. 'Good, isn't it? But I'm not thinking about it. That's the trick, Grandma – not to think about it. I learned it with the snowman. Just talk and let the words come out. Don't try to make them.'

James went on with his story, and the words kept flowing. 'The owl saw us flying back, and saw us landing. We don't do landings very well – they're a bit bumpy. But this flying, Grandma – *you* should do it. It's amazing! It's brilliant! It's really cool!'

'Well, I'm not sure I'm really dressed for it, dear,' she said rather nervously.

'Nor was James, and nor was I,' said the snowman. 'But if you'd like to go up for a spin, I'd be only too happy to take you.'

'Aren't I a bit heavy?' Grandma asked, still nervous, but also a bit excited now too.

'Not at all,' the snowman told her. 'You'll be fine up there. She'll be fine, won't she, James?'

'You'll love it, Grandma, I promise you,' James told her.

And he knew that he would love watching Grandma fly. And he did. He watched as the snowman put his arm round her and took off.

'My, oh my, oh my!' Grandma cried, waving down at James as she rose into the sky in her wellies, her dressing gown flapping. 'Will you look at me!'

James was looking at her all right. And what a sight it was! Grandma and the snowman flew down along the river, and away into the distance over the moors, till James could hardly see them. He wondered if his snowman was going to fly her all the way to see the Northern Lights at the North Pole, but soon they had circled round and were coming back towards him.

They landed just as James was hoping they would, bouncing and bumping along in the snow, and rolling over and over. Seeing Grandma somersaulting in her dressing gown and jimjams and wellies was the best, the absolute best! He ran over to them. They were both breathless and laughing with it all.

'Well,' said the snowman, standing up and helping James get Grandma up on her feet again. 'That was fun. But, to be honest, I think

I had better have a bit of a rest now. I'm rather tired after all that flying about. I sleep standing up, you know. All snowmen do.'

So back they all went to where James had first built his snowman. James and Grandma patted him all over where bits of snow had fallen away. 'You're missing another of your Brussels-sprout buttons,' James told him.

'I'll bring one out for you in the morning,' said Grandma. 'And thank you for my wonderful ride. It was the ride of a lifetime.'

'Mine was too,' James said. 'Sleep well, Mr Snowman.'

And they went away and left him, but James didn't want to go quite yet. He turned and ran back to his snowman, threw his arms round him and hugged him and hugged him. It was a hug he wanted to last forever.

'I think you gave me my voice,' he told the snowman. 'I can talk like other people now.'

'So can I,' said the snowman. 'So you gave me my voice too. See you in the morning, James,' he went on. 'Off you go now. It's Christmas Day, you know. The sun will be up soon. You get some sleep. And have the best time this Christmas, James.'

'Happy Christmas, Mr Snowman,' James said, and off he ran to catch up with Grandma, stopping to wave to his snowman from time to time. And each time his snowman waved back.

Then, with one last wave, one last look at his snowman, he was through the door and climbing the stairs to his bedroom. It had been a long, long night.

Grandma snuggled him down and told him that, thanks to him and his snowman, this was already by far the best Christmas she had ever had, or was ever likely to have.

'Same for me, Grandma,' James said, and he was fast asleep before he knew it.

Chapter Fifteen

As James slept that night, he dreamed that Father Christmas came flying over his house in his sleigh, the bells jingling, the reindeer puffing and panting and snorting because they had come so far and so fast. He dreamed that Father Christmas was coming down the chimney with a sack full of presents over his shoulder, and tiptoeing past Bertie, who was growling at him from his basket.

Then he was leaving lots of presents by the Christmas tree, and coming up the stairs, creakily, into James's bedroom, and filling up the stocking that Dad had left out on the end of the bed. His chubby face and red suit and white beard were covered in soot, but he was still smiling. He didn't seem to mind.

As quickly as Father Christmas had come, he was gone again, and James could hear the jingling of the bells and the puffing and panting and snorting of the reindeer. 'Giddy up, my beauties!' he heard from outside. 'Giddy up! Happy Christmas, James! Happy Christmas!' And the last of the jingling bells faded away into the night.

James woke up. It was day. Grandma was calling out, 'Happy Christmas, everyone!' It was Christmas Day! And there was his stocking

at the end of the bed, stuffed full.

James was out of bed quick as a twick. He snatched up his stocking and ran across the hallway to Grandma's room, bumping into Mum and Dad, both carrying their stockings, both looking sleepy. And then, as they did every Christmas, they all climbed on to Grandma's bed to open their stockings. Bertie had jumped up and was busy licking himself. He was allowed on beds on Christmas Day.

Soon the bed was covered in torn wrapping paper, and chocolates, and socks, and gloves, and a drying-up cloth, and books, and a toy racer, and a packet of jelly babies, and a key ring with a red bus dangling from the end, and lavender soap for Grandma, and talcum powder for Mum, and aftershave for Dad, a David Bowie CD for Mum, and a DVD of *Mamma Mia* for

Grandma, and another of *Paddington* for James, and more chocolates, and lots, lots more.

It wasn't long before all the unwrapping was over and they were all contentedly sitting on Grandma's bed scoffing their tangerines, which were always the last thing they pulled out of the very bottom of their stockings.

That was when Dad said – as he always did on Christmas morning after the stockings had been opened and the tangerines eaten: 'Well, James, I wonder what Father Christmas has left for us downstairs under the Christmas tree!'

James was first downstairs. As he searched through the presents, his heart sank. There was nothing nearly big enough to be a mountain bike; nothing the right shape. He had a pencil case from Mum, a woolly hat from someone – he'd already forgotten who – a pair of bright red wellies from Dad, and a hand-knitted jumper from Grandma, but no mountain bike. No mountain bike.

He was trying very hard not to look disappointed when Mum said, 'You do have one more little present, James. Father Christmas told us he hated wrapping it. *It's a bit of an awkward shape,* he said. So he just tied a ribbon round it and left it in the hall. Your dad'll fetch it in – won't you, dear?'

That was when Dad got up and, with the broadest of smiles on his face, went out of the room. Grandma told James to close his eyes. He did, but then he cheated and looked through his fingers. When Dad came back in, he was wheeling a bike; a bright green mountain bike with big fat tyres!

James jumped and down, laughing and

clapping his hands with joy. He said 'Thank you' and hugged everyone again and again. Bertie went bonkers, barking his silly head off and chasing his tail. And of course Grandma cried, which she often did when she was happy.

'I'm going to ride it right now. It's got big fat tyres. It'll go in the snow. I'm going to show my snowman,' James said, already wheeling the bike

out of the room. Just before he left, he turned to his parents and said: 'Do you like my words? They were the snowman's present. He gave me words.'

Before they could say anything, and before they could stop him, he was through the front door and out of the house, still in his pyjamas. Then he was jumping on his bike and cycling away through the snow. There wasn't nearly as much snow now as there had been the day before, but even so the bike slipped and slid around as James cycled across the garden, past the duck pond, through the gate and out into Oak Tree Field.

'Look what I've got, Mr Snowman!' he cried, struggling to control his slithering wheels in the slush and snow. 'Look what Father Christmas brought me!'

And then James looked up. His snowman was nowhere to be seen. He looked all around. He was gone! His snowman had gone!

James got off his bike, dropped it in the snow and ran over to where the snowman had been. All that was left of him was a pile of snow, a couple of Brussels sprouts, a tangerine, two apples, the green scarf and Dad's old hat.

James ran out into the field, calling and calling for him. 'Come back, Mr Snowman! Come back! I need you, Mr Snowman! I want to show you my bike. Please come back, come back!'

He listened for an answer, but there was none – only the crows cawing from above him, only the ducks quacking from the pond. James had lost his best friend, and suddenly he felt all alone in the world. He didn't cry; he was too sad even for that.

Then Grandma was beside him, her arm round him. 'He'll be back, James,' she said. 'The next time it snows you can make him all over again. So you haven't lost him. He's just gone away for a while, that's all. Didn't he give us a good time, James? Didn't he give us the best time ever? You won't forget; I won't forget; he won't forget. He'll be back next Christmas probably – maybe before, whenever the snow comes again. And the snow always comes again, doesn't it? So he will too. You'll see.'

Afterword

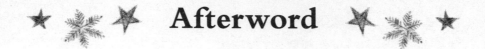

When it was first suggested to me that I might retell Raymond Briggs's *The Snowman* as a novella, I thought it was not a good idea at all. Here is a book known and loved by millions. It has no words because it did not need any words. So no, don't do it, leave it alone. The book is iconic, quite wonderful enough as it is.

Then I watched the film of it again. There was animation, there was music, and the story was not exactly the same. And it was a great film, one that has become as much loved as the book. So then I thought again. Isn't it a fine idea to tell the story in different ways? It has been filmed. There was a book of the film. It has been often adapted for the stage, seen by hundreds of thousands, and acted out in school plays no doubt. And families still love Raymond Briggs's original book. Indeed, maybe more of them have discovered it since the trip to the theatre, since seeing the film, since acting in the school play. So why not write a novella! It's a beautiful story. I will ask

Raymond Briggs if it's all right with him, and it was. I will keep the spirit and tone of his story, but simply try to tell it out my way.

I have to tell you I loved writing it. I sat in my shed on wheels in my garden, a sort of shepherd's hut, and told it down, writing, as I always do, by hand. I imagined I was telling it to an audience of children who probably knew and loved the story already, as much as I did. So I had them on my side from the start, and they listened to every word, the pictures already in their heads. I was hardly aware I was writing at all. I was enjoying my storymaking so much.

So thank you, Mr Briggs, for your story, for letting me tell it my way, and thank you, Puffin, for suggesting it. Good idea, great idea!

Michael Morpurgo

Michael Morpurgo

Michael Morpurgo has written over 130 books, many of them award-winning. His best-known work, *War Horse*, was adapted into a multi-Oscar-nominated film by Steven Spielberg, and into a widely acclaimed play. With his wife Clare, he set up the charity Farms for City Children, and for their pioneering work they were both awarded the MBE in 1999. In 2003 Michael became the third Children's Laureate, a position he helped to create with the poet Ted Hughes. In 2017 he was awarded a knighthood for services to literature and charity.

Raymond Briggs

Raymond Briggs is one of our most
respected and beloved artists. He has
created characters that are now icons
for generations of children, including
Fungus the Bogeyman, *Father Christmas*
and, of course, the beloved *Snowman*.
He has won many awards over his career
including the Kurt Maschler Award, the
Children's Book of the Year, the Dutch
Silver Pen Award, and the prestigious
Kate Greenaway Award twice. In 2017
Raymond was awarded the BookTrust
Lifetime Achievement Award.

Raymond's original cover sketch

The
Snowman

through the ages . . .

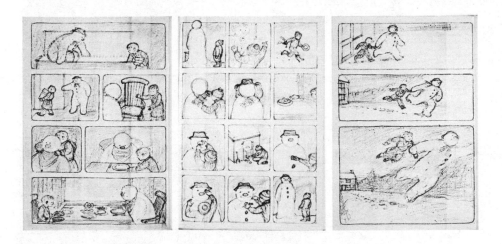

Raymond Briggs's wordless classic picture book, *The Snowman*, was first published in 1978 and has gone on to sell over 5.5 million copies around the world. The story has inspired films, music, a stage play and a sequel. For many families, Christmas wouldn't be Christmas without *The Snowman*.

The Snowman was the
fifth picture book created
by Raymond Briggs, who
also wrote and illustrated
Father Christmas and
Fungus the Bogeyman.

Unusually *The Snowman*
is wordless, and told
entirely through pictures.

Raymond never intended for *The Snowman* to be a festive
tale and the original story does not mention Christmas.
Neither does it feature Father Christmas or a Christmas tree!

Producer John Coates created a 26-minute animated version of *The Snowman*, which was first broadcast by Channel 4 on Boxing Day 1982. Channel 4 has shown the film every Christmas since.

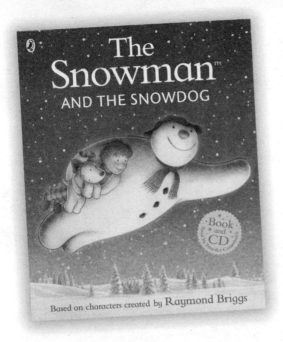

A sequel, *The Snowman and the Snowdog*, was created to celebrate 30 years of the classic film and was premiered on Channel 4 on Christmas Eve 2012.

Christmas Traditions Around the World

Iceland

People in Iceland will often exchange books on Christmas Eve, then spend the rest of the night reading them and eating chocolate. The tradition is part of a season called *Jolabokaflod*, or 'The Christmas Book Flood'.

Bolivia

Bolivians celebrate *Misa del Gallo* ('Mass of the Rooster') on Christmas Eve, with people bringing roosters to midnight mass to symbolize the belief that the bird was the first animal to announce the birth of Jesus Christ.

⭐ Germany

St Nikolaus travels by donkey in the middle of the night on 6 December and leaves little treats like coins, chocolate, oranges and toys in the shoes of good German children. But St Nikolaus often brings along Knecht Ruprecht – a devil-like character dressed in dark clothes covered with bells – who punishes any children who misbehave.

⭐ Greenland

Greenland's traditional Christmas dish, *kiviak*, takes a full seven months to prepare. It begins with hollowing out a seal skin and stuffing it with 500 auks – a seabird – to ferment. When the holiday comes around, the dish is served straight from the seal.

Poland

Spider webs are common Christmas-tree decorations in Poland because, according to legend, a spider weaved a blanket for Baby Jesus. Many Polish people consider spiders to be symbols of goodness and prosperity.

Mexico

'The Night of the Radishes' is one of the annual Christmas customs in Oaxaca, Mexico. On 23 December, competitors carve nativity scenes into large radishes, which are proudly displayed at the Christmas market.

Norway

Norway has a tradition that dates back centuries to when people believed that witches and evil spirits came out on Christmas Eve looking for brooms to ride on. To this day, many people still hide their brooms in the safest place in the house to stop them from being stolen.

Colombia

Día de las Velitas marks the start of the Christmas season across Colombia. In honour of the Virgin Mary and the Immaculate Conception, people place candles and paper lanterns in their windows, balconies and front gardens.

Peru

In Peru, 24 December is the main day for celebrations. After mass, families go home to feast, open gifts and toast each other at midnight. The most important decorations are *pesebre* – nativity scenes intricately carved from wood or stone. Gifts are spread around a manger rather than a tree, and it's considered lucky to be the one chosen to put the figurine of baby Jesus into the manger on Christmas Eve.

How to build the perfect snowman

James works all day to create his perfect snowman.
You might be able to bring an amazing snowman to life
too if you follow these top tips!

1. Wait for the right kind of snow.

You need snow that's wet and packable, not powdery or fluffy. Pick some up and press it between your hands – if it makes a ball, you'll be able to make a snowman. If the snow falls apart, it's no good – and you might have to wait for the next snowfall!

2. Find a flat section of grass in a shady spot.

If you build your snowman on a slope, it could topple over. Make sure the area has plenty of snow for you to use. If you want your snowman to last as long as possible without melting, build it somewhere that doesn't get much sunshine.

3. Put on warm clothes.

You'll need warm waterproof gloves and boots, and warm layers of clothing. You don't want to get too cold to finish your work!

4. Make a big snowball for the bottom of the snowman.

Add snow to a snowball in your hands until it gets too big to hold and then roll the ball along the ground to collect more snow. Make sure you keep pushing in different directions to collect snow on all sides. Pat it as you go to press the snow down. When it's big enough, roll the ball to where you want to build your snowman.

5. Make the middle of the snowman.

Start with another large snowball and roll it on the ground again. Make sure you don't make it too heavy to lift! When you are ready, lift the middle section on to the bottom section.

6. Make a snowball for the head.

When you've got a third snowball to the right size to be your
snowman's head, carefully place it on top of the snowman's
body. You could smooth down the sides of the middle section
to make arms for your snowman.

Decorate your snowman!

Your snowman will need a nose.

Will you use a carrot or a tangerine?
If you have something else that you
think would look cool as a nose,
use that instead.

**Choose your
snowman's eyes.**

You could use stones,
coal or bouncy balls!
Push them into the
head and twist them
in a circle so that they
stick in the snow.

Make a mouth

You could use a row of stones, draw a
smile with your finger like James does
or even stick some plastic teeth in!

The rest is up to you!

Do you want to give your snowman arms
of twigs? Or decorate it with a scarf, hat,
feather boa, tie or sunglasses?

If you only have a little dusting of snow, why not
make a mini snowman with twigs for arms and
pebbles for eyes? You could even put it in a plastic
box and keep it 'alive' in the freezer all year round.

Have you read Raymond Briggs's wordless classic picture book?